Mother Duck
had three eggs.

One day the eggs
went – **Crack!**

Crack!

Crock!

Out came ...
one duckling.

Out came another duckling. Out came ...

... something green!
"Funny duckling!"
said Mother Duck.

9

"So ... scaly!"

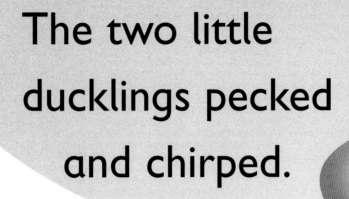

The two little ducklings pecked and chirped.

The third
one went ...

13

...snap!

"No snapping!"
said Mother Duck.

The funny duckling
ran away, all alone.

But then he found
other green ducklings.

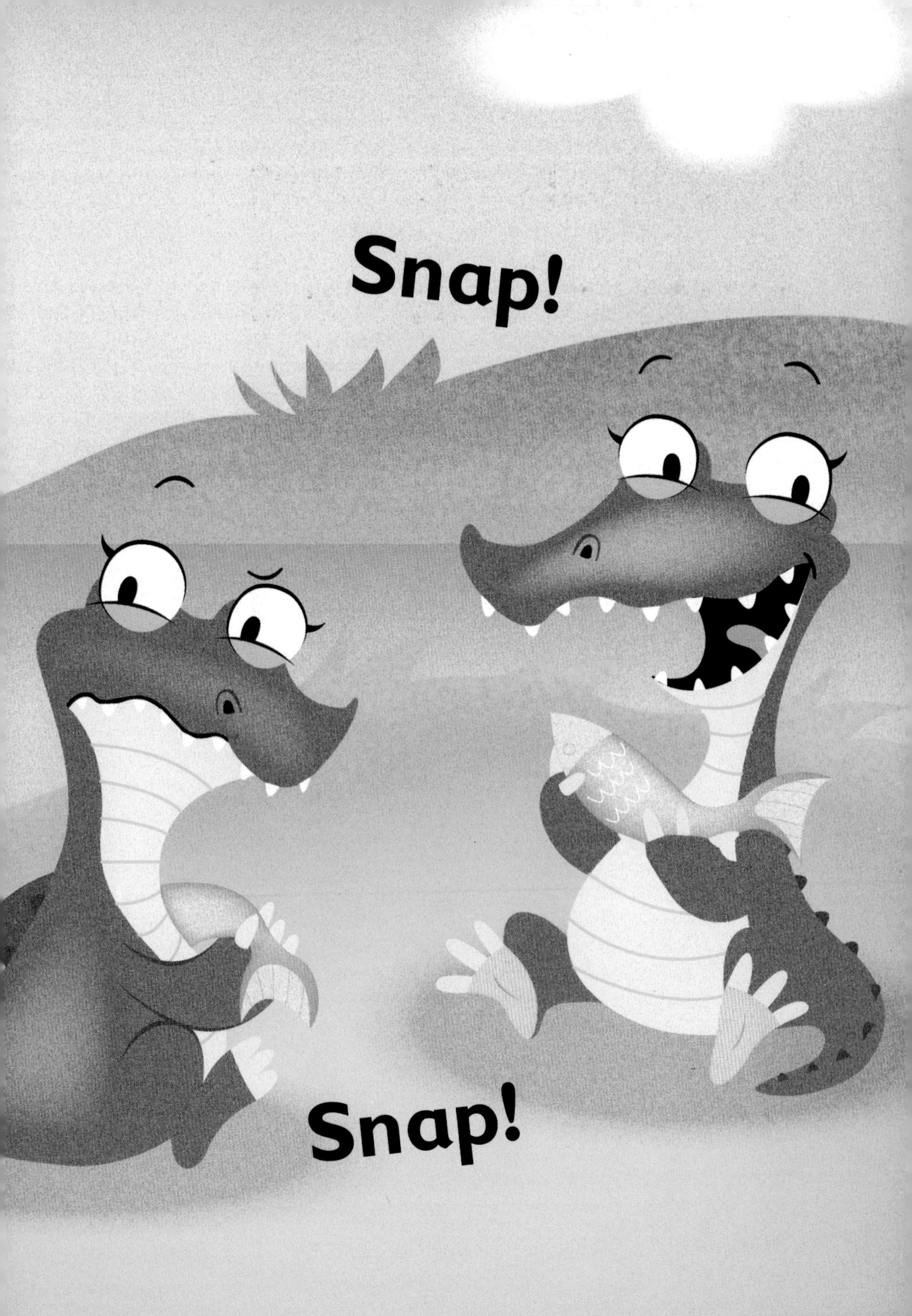

Snap!

Snap!

"Will you be my mother?" he asked. "Yes!" snapped Mother Croc.

Puzzle Time!

 a

 b

 c

 d

 e

 f

Put these pictures in the right
order and tell the story!

playful

careful

excited

worried

Which words describe Croc and which describe Mother Duck?

Turn over for answers!

Notes for adults

TADPOLES are structured to provide support for newly independent readers. The stories may also be used by adults for sharing with young children.

Starting to read alone can be daunting. **TADPOLES** help by providing visual support and repeating words and phrases. These books will both develop confidence and encourage reading and rereading for pleasure.

If you are reading this book with a child, here are a few suggestions:

1. Make reading fun! Choose a time to read when you and the child are relaxed and have time to share the story.
2. Talk about the story before you start reading. Look at the cover and the blurb. What might the story be about? Why might the child like it?
3. Encourage the child to retell the story, using the jumbled picture puzzle as a starting point. Extend vocabulary with the matching words to characters puzzle.
4. Give praise! Remember that small mistakes need not always be corrected.

Answers

Here is the correct order:

1.c 2.b 3.a 4.f 5.e 6.d

Words to describe Croc:
excited, playful

Words to describe
Mother Duck:
careful, worried